LETTERS
from the
CANYON

For my children, Megan and Ryan Boyd,
who travelled halfway around the world
to be the center of my universe.

I would like to gratefully acknowledge the assistance of
Pam Frazier, Colleen Hyde, Sara Stebbins,
Jeanne Pendergast, Greer Price, Mike Quinn, Kim Besom,
Martha Suzanne Davis-Weatherill, Greer Chesher,
Mary Devine, Dave Toole, Kim Buchheit, Lea Tuck,
Chuck and Sally Wahler, Maralyn Miller, M.K.Callan
and the loving spirit of Karen L.Taylor.

Thank you also to my husband, Jim Boyd,
for discouraging any swan dives off the Rim.

LETTERS
from the
CANYON

AN ALPHABETICAL VISIT TO THE GRAND CANYON

Text, Calligraphy and Illustrations
by
Kathleen McAnally

3 1336 05858 8501

GRAND CANYON ASSOCIATION

This book belongs to

_____

First Edition

Printed on recycled paper using soy inks.
Manufactured in Hong Kong.

ISBN 0-938216-52-X
Library of Congress Catalog Card Number 95-078447

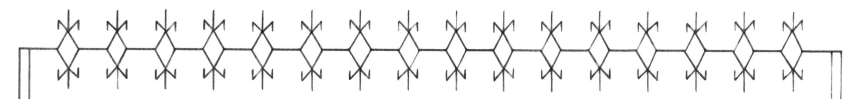

Every passing cloud, every change in the position
of the sun, recasts the whole.   C.E. Dutton

Introduction

The changing spectacle of beauty and life surrounding
the Grand Canyon has amazed and enchanted people for
thousands of years. This book offers an introduction to
the history and natural resources of this unique area.

The border designs used throughout the book were
inspired by the beautiful artwork of the Navajo and Hopi
peoples who are native to this region. Waiting to be
discovered on each page is at least one unidentified item
whose name begins with the appropriate letter. A list of
these may be found in the Postscript at the end of the
book. Watch for them on every page!

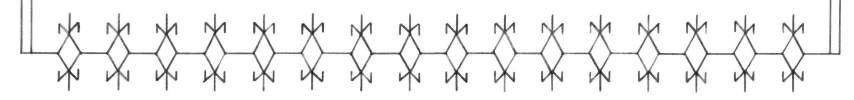

Nevada

Utah

Colorado

New Mexico

California

Arizona, the Grand Canyon state, shares borders with five other states and the country of Mexico.

Anasazi is a name given to the ancestors of the Pueblo peoples who lived in this area about 800 years ago.

The tall flowering spike of the **Agave** looks like a giant white candle.

Mexico

NATIONAL PARK SERVICE

National Park Service personnel from all over the country attend a variety of classes offered by **Albright Training Center** at Grand Canyon.

A

The **Backcountry Office** issues permits to **Backpackers** for camping in the Canyon.

Lucky hikers will forget their **Blisters** when they share the trail with **Bighorn Sheep**.

Bats help to control the insect population.

The two **Bridges** at the bottom of the Canyon allow people and mules to cross the river.

The **Colorado River** flows through the bottom of the Canyon.

The famous architect **Mary Colter** designed many of the beautiful buildings at Grand Canyon.

The lovely, fragrant **Cliff Rose** appears to be a bush of tiny feathers when the flowers turn to seeds.

The spectacular views from **Cedar Ridge** are only one and a half miles down the South Kaibab Trail.

C

Hermits Rest was named
for Louis D. Boucher,
a French Canadian
miner who lived
for several years
at the tiny oasis of
Dripping Springs.

The many Mule Deer in the Park
get their name from their large ears.

Mary Colter's
Indian Watchtower
is located at
Desert View,
the east entrance to the Park.

The Canyon
is 1 mile Deep

but 7 ½ miles

Down
by trail.

D

When the exclusive **El Tovar** opened in 1905 it had its own dairy herd for milk, chickens for eggs and gardens on the roof. Rooms cost $4 to $6 a night.

The stately **Elk** is the largest mammal in the Park. It is also known as Wapiti, from a Shawnee word which means white rump.

The Grand Canyon was formed through millions of years of **Erosion** by wind and water. Loose rocks, caused by this erosion, can make the **Edge** of the Canyon dangerous.

E

Fred Harvey, an Englishman who moved to America in 1850, built a chain of restaurants and hotels along the Santa Fe Railway all across the West.

Fossil imprints of plants and animals that lived here millions of years ago can be found in the Canyon walls.

Fires caused by lightning are one of nature's tools for recycling.

In the 1890s visitors to the Canyon spent eleven hours riding the stagecoach from the city of **Flagstaff**.

F

The Grand Canyon has amazed people with its tremendous size and beauty since they first saw it thousands of years ago. The Canyon was known to the Paiute people by the beautiful word "Kaibab" (Kī bab) which means "mountain lying down."

The pink coloring of the
Grand Canyon Rattlesnake
helps it to blend in with the colors of the Canyon.

Adventurous young women who worked at the
Fred Harvey restaurants along the Santa Fe
Railway from the 1880s to the 1950s were
called **Harvey Girls**.

The **Havasupai** (which means people of the
blue-green water) live near **Havasu Falls**
at the bottom of the Canyon.

At the far end of West Rim
Drive **Hermits Rest**
offers travelers a shady
spot for refreshments.

Miner, trailbuilder, postmaster, tourist
guide and gifted storyteller,
John Hance built the first
tent camp "hotel" on the rim near Grandview.

The rocks of the **Inner Gorge** are the oldest in the Canyon and almost half the age of the Earth.

Indian Garden, 4 ½ miles down the Bright Angel Trail, was once the home of a band of Havasupai whose crops were watered from the spring.

The Park Rangers who teach people  about nature, history and the environment are called **Interpreters**.

East of the Park the historic trading post of Cameron offers a delicious local favorite, the **Indian Taco**.

Green Chilis
Tomatoes
Cheese
Lettuce
Pinto Beans
Fry Bread
Plate

I

Children who wish to learn more about the Park and caring for its resources may take part in the

Junior Ranger Program.

The remarkably blue Steller's Jay has a crest on top of its black head.

The Kaibab Squirrel, found only on the North Rim of the Grand Canyon, has long hair called tassels on the edges of its ears. Its cousin, the Abert Squirrel, lives on the South Rim.

The Kolb Brothers photographed tourists riding mules down the Bright Angel Trail from a studio window hanging over the Canyon rim.

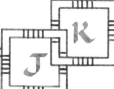

Layers of the Earth's surface are exposed by the Canyon.

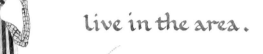

live in the area.

Many kinds of **Lizards**

Lupine and **Larkspur** are two of the beautiful wildflowers found near both the North and South Rims.

Lees Ferry

was a place for the early pioneer settlers to cross the river.

L

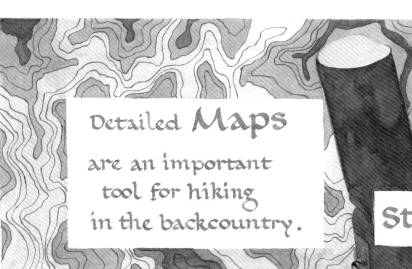

Detailed **Maps** are an important tool for hiking in the backcountry.

The first view of the Canyon for many visitors is from **Mather Point,** named for **Stephen T. Mather,** the first director of the National Park Service.

The edible bulbs of the **Mariposa Lily** were a source of food for the Navajo and Hopi peoples.

The famous **Mules,** or "long-eared taxis," of Grand Canyon wear studded horseshoes in winter just as cars use studded snowtires.

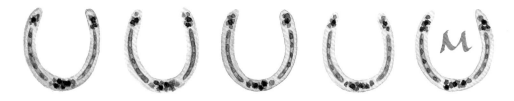

Beauty and history are preserved for everyone to enjoy in the **National Parks.**

Grand Canyon National Park was established on February 26, 1919.

High in the cliffs above the Colorado River, **Nankoweap Granaries** served as a place to store food for the Anasazi.

The higher elevation and greater moisture of the **North Rim** allow many plants to grow which are not often found on the South Rim.

N

The acorns of the Gambel Oak provide food for many animals.

Originally claimed as a copper mine in 1893, the Orphan Mine on the West Rim later produced uranium until 1966.

A short way down the South Kaibab Trail a large jumble of boulders known as Ooh-Aah Point is a favorite overlook of hikers.

The bark of a **Ponderosa Pine** turns orange as the tree grows older.

People who travel to the bottom of the Grand Canyon may rest beneath the cottonwood trees at **Phantom Ranch**.

Petroglyphs are picture stories carved in the rocks by people of long ago.

In the 1800s **Prospectors** and their burros searched the Canyon for gold.

Major John Wesley Powell led the first scientific expedition down the Colorado River in 1869.

P

The beautiful groves of
Quaking Aspen
on the North Rim often
share a common root
system, clone trees
springing up from the
roots like crabgrass.

Islands of **Shinumo Quartzite**,
a billion years old, lie buried deep in the
Canyon beneath the Tapeats Sandstone
which formed at the bottom of
an ancient ocean.

 **Park Rangers** instruct and protect visitors to the National Parks.

Magnificent **Red Butte** towers above the Kaibab National Forest south of the Canyon.

All the water used in the Village on the South Rim comes from **Roaring Springs** on the cliffs of the North Rim.

River Runners guide the **Raft** adventures through the **Rapids** on the Colorado River.

Using the **Recycle Containers** in the Park helps to save the **Resources** of our planet.

In the summer it's fun to ride the **Shuttlebus** around the Village and it helps to reduce traffic in the Park.

4000 years ago (long before the Anasazi), people of the Desert Archaic culture placed willow and cottonwood **Split-twig Figurines** in caves of the Canyon.

In 1901 a **Santa Fe Railroad Steam Engine** pulled the first train passengers to the Canyon from Williams.

Known to the Navajo people as the **Song Dog,** the coyote often fills the night with his eerie yips and howls.

The **Tonto Trail** wanders for 95 miles along the **Tonto Platform** halfway down the Canyon. The North Kaibab, South Kaibab and Bright Angel **Trails** are the most popular in the Park and are known as the Corridor.

Wild **Turkeys** feed in the meadows during the day and sleep in the trees at night.

Displays about peoples who have lived in this area may be seen at the **Tusayan Ruins** near Desert View.

Small animals like the
Uinta Chipmunk
become snacks for
larger animals when
people fatten them
up with human
junk food.

Hiking back
Up
out of the
Canyon takes
twice as long
as going down.

Unkar Delta on the
Colorado River below Desert View
provided the Anasazi with food,
water and homesites for
over 200 years.

The tiny blue
cone of the
Utah Juniper
looks like a
berry and is a
popular food
with animals.

Every year millions of Visitors travel from all over the world to see the Grand Canyon.

The tallest of the San Francisco Peaks near Flagstaff is one of many ancient Volcanoes in the area.

Vishnu Temple is one of many Canyon features whose name refers to a God in the mythology of another country.

The most important thing to take on a hike in the Canyon is plenty of **Water**.

The **Wranglers** who lead the mule trains in and out of the Canyon are called trail guides.

The enchanting **Widforss Trail** on the North Rim was named for **Gunnar Widforss**, an artist who created beautiful watercolors of the Canyon in the 1920s.

Softly falling, heavy snows blanket both rims in the **Winter** and close the North Rim for the season.

The common flicker is a **Woodpecker** who enjoys feeding on ants in the ground.

Landscaping with plants
that need very little
water is called

Xeriscaping.

People have used fruits of the YUCCA plant
for food, roots for soap, and leaf fibers for
making ropes, baskets and sandals.

The murals beneath the huge
windows at the

Yavapai Observation Station

allow visitors to identify
Canyon landmarks.

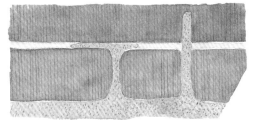

Striped areas of pink **Zoroaster Granite** at the bottom of the Canyon entered the darker Vishnu schist as molten rock billions of years ago.

Zuni Point on East Rim Drive was named for an American Indian tribe known for their beautiful stonework. Their language is unrelated to any other in the Southwest.

Certain plants and animals thrive at different elevations or **Life Zones**. The desert life of the Inner Gorge is not like that of the pine forests above the Rims.

Z

Postscript

 Hoary Aster

Bluebells

 Cushion Cactus

 Chuckwalla

 Arizona Mountain Dandelion

 White Tufted Evening-primrose

 Blue Flax

 Globemallow Great Horned Owl Goldenweed

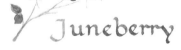 Hummingbird Horsetail Indian Corn

 Juneberry Kissing Bug Specklepod Locoweed

 Leaves  Monarch Butterfly  Pigmy Nuthatch Ore

Yellow Owl-clover

Oldman-whiskers

Pick

Desert Phlox

Pine Needles

Gambel's Quail

Common Raven

Sacred Datura

Scorpion

Tarantula

Tusayan Flame Flower (endangered)

Yellow Umbrellaplant

Virginia's Warbler

Tall Verbena

Solitary Vireo

Canada Violet

Long-tailed Vole

Wow

Watercolors

Xylem

Western Yarrow

Yellow Jacket

Zion Buckwheat

Katie McAnally received a BFA degree

in Graphic Arts from Colorado State University, and

later attended Montana State University, earning a degree

in Art Education. She has since worked as a free lance artist,

studying with numerous internationally recognized calligraphers.

She has lived for several years with her family in

Grand Canyon National Park.